InVentor McGregor

Kathleen T. Pelley

Pictures by Michael Chesworth

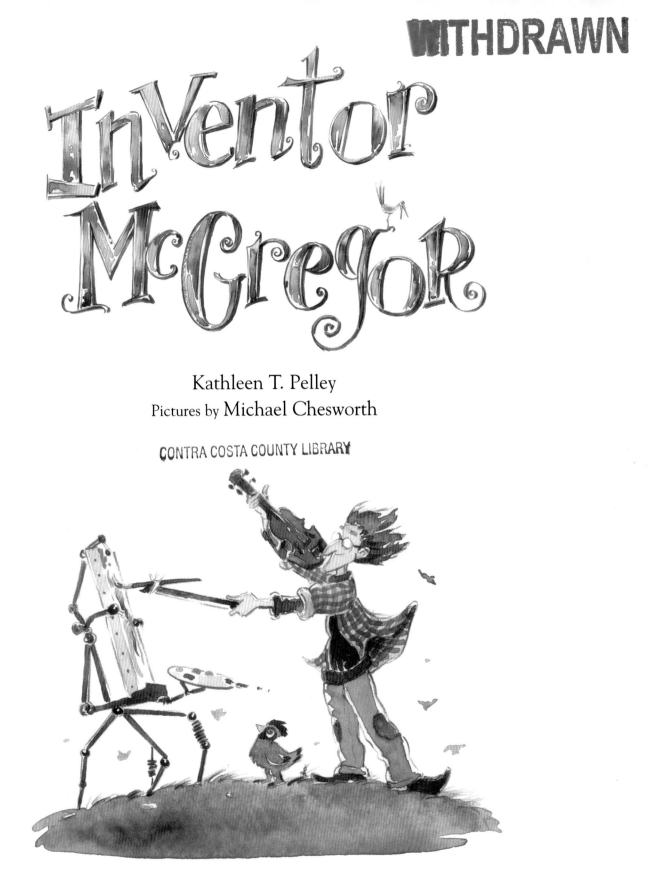

Farrar Straus Giroux • New York

For my daughters, Meghan and Roisin—the heart of my happy, happy home
—K.P.

For Howard Roark
—M.C.

Text copyright © 2006 by Kathleen T. Pelley
Illustrations copyright © 2006 by Michael Chesworth
Distributed in Canada by Douglas & McIntyre Ltd.
Color separations by Chroma Graphics PTE Ltd.
Printed and bound in the United States of America by Phoenix Color Corporation
Designed by Jay Colvin
First edition, 2006
10 9 8 7 6 5 4 3 2 1

www.fsgkidsbooks.com

Library of Congress Cataloging-in-Publication Data
Pelley, Kathleen.
    Inventor McGregor / Kathleen T. Pelley ; pictures by
Michael Chesworth.— 1st ed.
        p.   cm.
    Summary: Hector McGregor, inventor of peppermint
pencils, glow-in-the-dark books, and other unusual items,
leaves his home workshop to work in a laboratory but finds
that his inspiration comes from being around his cheery wife,
five children, and a hen called Hattie.
    ISBN-13: 978-0-374-33606-6
    ISBN-10: 0-374-33606-7
    [1. Inventors—Fiction.   2. Family life—Fiction.
3. Home—Fiction.   4. Humorous stories.]   I. Chesworth,
Michael, ill.   II. Title.

PZ7.P3645In 2006
[E]—dc22
                                    2004046944

Hector McGregor lived in a higgledy-piggledy
house with a cheery wife, five children, and a hen called Hattie.

Mend-It McGregor, everyone called him, because he could mend most anything that needed mending, they said, from fishing rods and fairy wands to top hats and rubber ducks. Day after day people brought him their squeaky skates, squiggly spoons, wobbly wagons, tangled kites, knotted yo-yos, headless dolls, and footless soldiers. With a blob of glue or a squirt of oil, with a tap of his hammer or a shimmy here and a shimmy there, Hector McGregor fixed whatever needed fixing, and sent everyone on their way with a skip, a hop, and a hum.

In between his gluing and oiling and hammering, Hector McGregor liked to stroll down the winding lane at the back of his house where the bluebells grew and the smell of wet heather lingered long and sweet. There he sang a snippet of a song or twirled a whirl of a fling, or sometimes he pulled out his palette and his easel to paint a picture. Then back to his work he went with a heart that was both happy and full.

And every night before the shades were drawn, Hector McGregor nestled his fiddle beneath his chin and played a rousing reel or a sweeping strathspey, while all around the house, from pantry to parlor, his cheery wife, his five children, and his hen called Hattie whirled and whooshed and wheeched.

One day Angus, the postman, stopped by to have his bag patched. "That wee scoundrel of a Scottie down Loopy Lane has torn it to tatters again," he grumbled.

"Dear me," said Hector McGregor. "We need to stop that scallywag. Leave it to me. I'll think of something."

The next day Hector McGregor handed Angus a shiny new bag covered
with all sorts of buttons, dangling cords, and flapping flaps.

"What's this?" asked Angus.

"It's a barking bag," said Hector McGregor. "Whenever you see that
Scottie, just push this button and flip this flap, and it'll set off a barking
noise as loud as a hundred wolfhounds."

With his new bag slung over his shoulder, Angus, the postman, went on
his way. By the end of the day the whole town had heard the story of how
the barking bag had sent the Scottie fleeing with his tail between his legs.

Now everyone wanted Hector McGregor to concoct some thingamabob or thingamajig to make their world a little better or brighter. When Mrs. MacKay complained about her boys who dawdled and dillydallied all the way to school, Hector McGregor crafted detachable monkey tails so they could swing and swoop and swish their way through the treetops.

To lighten the children's schoolbags, he invented a paper pump that blew up their books with helium. Now down the road they sauntered clutching their books above them like a bunch of bobbing balloons.

For Mrs. McIver, who had triplets and a husband at sea, Hector McGregor pieced together some helping hands that she could strap to her shoulder. Every morning, with a flick of a switch, off they went wiping noses, zipping zippers, tying laces, and holding hands.

For Jamie Campbell, who always slept through his alarm clock, Hector McGregor built an alarm bed that popped his head from the pillow like a Jack from his box.

And for wee Willie Beattie, the smallest boy in his class, Hector McGregor cobbled a pair of bouncing boots so that he could see over walls and fences and heads.

Inventor McGregor everyone called him now because he could invent most anything that needed inventing, they said. And in between his ideas simmering and sparking, Hector McGregor still liked to stroll down the winding lane at the back of his house where the bluebells grew and the smell of wet heather lingered long and sweet. There he sang his snippet of a song, painted a picture, or twirled a whirl of a fling.

One day the president of the Royal Society of Inventors, Nigel Withers, paid Hector McGregor a visit. "Congratulations, Mr. McGregor," he said. "We're so impressed with all your inventions that we'd like you to become a member of our society. We want you to start working for us immediately in your very own laboratory in the city."

"Why, thank you," said Hector McGregor. "But I don't think I'll need a laboratory. You see, I like working here where I can sing and paint and—"

"Oh no, no, no!" protested Mr. Withers. "Real inventors don't have time for all that nonsense. They invent—that's all. Just imagine how many more gadgets and gizmos you'll be able to think up with a clear head and no distractions."

Hector McGregor scratched his chin. "Hmm," he said. "Maybe you're right."

And the next week Hector McGregor
set off to work in the city in his very
own laboratory.

Mr. Withers gave
him a long white coat
and a badge that read

Inventor
McGregor

Outside his
door hung a sign
with the words

QUIET
INVENTOR
INVENTING

All day Hector McGregor sat at his drawing board in the laboratory thinking about what to invent. He thought and he thought and he thought. So long did he think that by the time he arrived home at night, all his children were sound asleep in bed, and his cheery wife sat dozing by the fire with Hattie the hen in her lap.

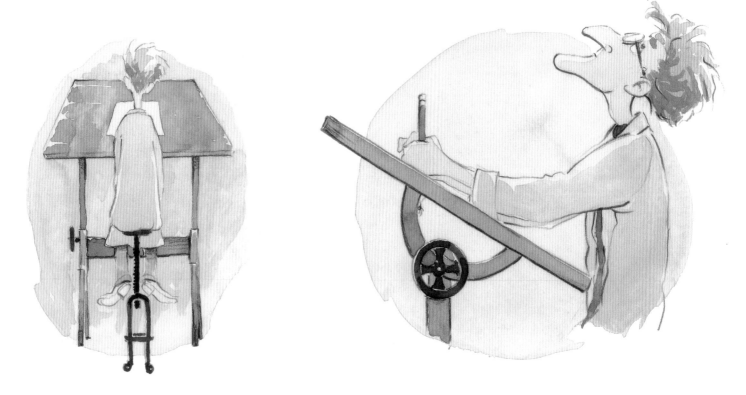

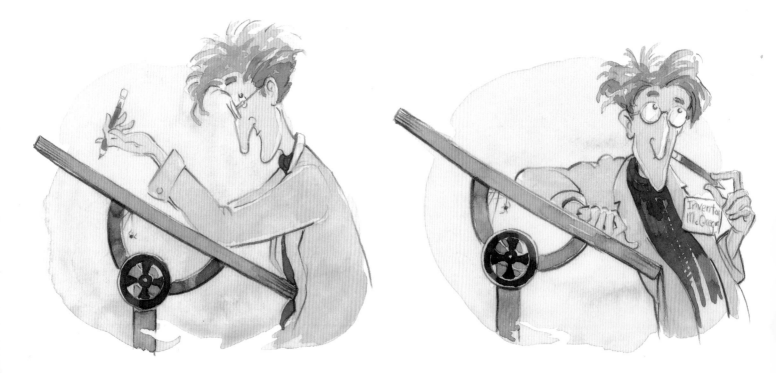

The next day was no different. Nor the next. Nor the one after that. Day after day, week after week, Hector McGregor sat at his drawing board in the laboratory staring out the window at the toy store across the street. He thought and he thought and he thought. But no matter how long or how hard he thought, no ideas came to him.

Soon people stopped calling him Inventor McGregor. Whenever he walked down the street, the people whispered to one another.

"It's sad."

"A mistake."

"Not a real inventor."

Hector McGregor hung his head in shame. Whenever Mr. Withers popped his head around the door of the laboratory, Hector McGregor saw the frown in his eyes. And again he hung his head in shame.

Maybe I'm not a real inventor, after all, he thought one day. Maybe I should give back my badge, my coat, and my laboratory. But as he was thinking this thought, he noticed some workers painting the toy store across the road. Suddenly an urge tickled down his arms and into his fingertips.

Up he bolted. Out the door he flew. Across the street he dashed. "Quick! Quick!" he cried. "I need to borrow your brushes and paint." Bewildered and befuddled, the men handed them over. Back to the laboratory raced Hector McGregor with the buckets dangling from his arms.

Clutching a brush in each hand, he began to slosh and swish the colors across the laboratory wall. Splish! Splash! Splosh!

First he painted a picture of his cheery wife sitting beneath the plum tree at the side of his house. Next came a picture of his five children paddling in the pond by the front gate. Finally Hattie, his hen, appeared, pecking her corn at the bottom of the winding lane.

Then Hector McGregor threw down his brushes and beamed at all the faces he loved splashed across the wall. With a hoot and a holler, he dashed out the door and flew down the street.

"Where are you going?" Mr. Withers called after him.

"Home to my happy, happy home," cried Hector McGregor.

Back at his higgledy-piggledy house, Hector McGregor kissed his cheery wife, his five children, and his hen called Hattie. He strolled down the winding lane behind his house where the bluebells grew and the smell of wet heather lingered long and sweet. There he sang a snippet of a song. He twirled a whirl of a fling.

And he painted a picture of a marmalade cat curled up in a patch of
sunlight. Then back to his inventing he went with a heart that was happy
and full.

Week after week, one more incredible invention after another spilled out
of him—peppermint pencils, doggie Wellingtons, jelly bean erasers, tartan
grass, mufflers to warm noses, and books that glowed in the dark. Inventor
McGregor everyone called him again, because he could invent most anything
that needed inventing, they said, just as long as he could sing and paint, and
fiddle and fling, and love all that he had to love.

And every night Inventor McGregor nestled his fiddle beneath his chin and played a rousing reel or a sweeping strathspey, while all around the house, from pantry to parlor, his cheery wife, his five children, and his hen called Hattie whirled and whooshed and wheeched.